I0783547

Written and illustrated by Joe Allgeier⬛
Edited by Leah Yurka
Printed in the United States of America
ISBN 979-8-9878318-2-3

Dedicated to JJ for all your amazing ideas for Kirby.

A special thanks to B, my greatest collaborator and best friend.

Each of Santa's elves is special in their own way, however, some elves really stand out and shine.

This was the case with Kirby the Elf.

As an elf in the Special Innovative Toys Sector (S.I.T.S. for short) of Santa's workshop, Kirby was known for creating the best toys. Each year, he would come up with a new toy, and the designs were made over and over, thousands of times, by the rest of the elves.

But each year as Christmas came closer, the head elf, Flick, would bear down more on S.I.T.S., urging the elves to come up with more toys, better toys, higher tech toys.

Flick
Ho Ho
Hold Your Complaints!
Til After
Christmas

His work had been magical at first, seeing his
work come to life and picturing the joy of a
child receiving one of his toys.
"The kids aren't impressed by the toys like
they used to be! They need to be enter-
tained, there needs to be more of everything.
They need action, digital, lights, screens!"

Video Games
Wooden Toys

Kirby slowly became more unhappy as he and the other elves worked feverishly each day in Santa's workshop. His favorite time of the day was when the last bell rang at quitting time, when he could go back to his small cottage at the edge of the village, and work on his own projects.

In his cottage, he would spend hours
working on his own toys, each design cre-
ated and made only once. These unique
toys were made of wood and lovingly
crafted, sanded, and painted, at his own
pace, in his own time.

Working on and making his own toys was what Kirby loved best of all, and every day he longed to sit next to the fire in his own workshop, creating and handcrafting his own work. There was no one telling him to make more, to work faster. He was alone with his own happy thoughts of the smiling children who would play with his toys.

One Day, Kirby looked around at his fellow S.I.T.S. elves working away, and realized that he had lost something. He had lost the Christmas spirit and the joy somewhere along the way working here in Santa's workshop. The times he truly felt happiest were when he was at home, working on his own creations.

He simply couldn't stay here anymore, working in S.I.T.S day after day, and being unhappy.

STOP
DAY
DREAMING
GAME
OVE

So Kirby nervously went to talk to
the big man, Mr. Claus.

17

He found Santa working, seated
behind his desk, which was covered
in stacks of papers and lists with
names and addresses.

Nice Naughty
Until Proven

Santa looked up as Kirby approached
the desk slowly. After the usual
hellos and how-are-yous were said, it
took a minute before Kirby got up the
courage to speak his mind.

"Do you remember when you first
started out and you made the toys
yourself?"

"Oh yes, of course," Santa smiled. "The world was a lot smaller then. I only made toys for the children in my small mountain village." The expression in Santa's eyes was happy and dreamy as he remembered. "I used to love the feeling of handing the toys to each child in person and watching them laugh as they played with my creations..."

He shook his head of the memories. "Of course, there is no time for that anymore, since the whole world wants more of everything."

The jolly man's words made Kirby feel even more sure of his decision, and his voice was hopeful as he finally said what he felt.

"Santa, I want to go back to that time. I
want to have my own workshop where I can
make my own handmade wooden toys, one
at a time, like you used to do."

After what seemed like a long time of Santa
staring in amazement at Kirby, he laughed
warmly.

"Kirby, you are an odd and wonderful elf,
and I admire you and your dream. But it
will be hard to go out on your own here at
the North Pole."

"You are right. That is why I have to
find the perfect place for me to make
my dream come true. Maybe
somewhere warm...".

Now Kirby was the one who was
silent as he saw the hole in his plan,
since he had no way to go anywhere
different.

Santa set his hand gently on Kirby's shoulder. "I think that I have a way to get you to someplace new and warm. Go see Stamp, the old elf who tends the dogs, near the reindeer stable. He can help you."

Santa Claus gave Kirby a big hug and one more smile. "Good luck, Kirby. I hope you'll find happiness at your new workshop."

Kirby found Stamp asleep, with one of
his dogs curled up next to him.

He gently woke Stamp up and told him of
his plan to leave the North Pole and
travel to a special, warm place to set up
his new workshop. "Will you help me?"

34

Stamp looked at Kirby curiously before he spoke. " Well, I am no fan of this cold since it makes my bones creak. Someplace warm sounds mighty fine, and if you will have my dogs, we can take you the whole way there."

"That sounds amazing." Kirby was
excited, but not sure of the next steps.

"How are two elves and eight dogs
going to travel that far? Can we fly
like Santa in his sleigh?"

Stamp shook his head and pointed at a heap covered by a tarp behind the shed. "Nowadays, everyone is flying around using sleighs and reindeer and the like. But back in my day, elves and even Santa used to travel by dog sled."

Kirby's eyes brightened as Stamp pulled off the tarp to reveal an old wooden sled.

"Now, if the dogs and I can remember
how to make this thing go...".

Stamp was thinking hard when the
dog that had been sleeping next to him
came up to him and rubbed her nose
against his hand.

41

"Oh, thank you Scout, I remember now," he said as he stroked the head of the big brown dog.

"First, I call each of the dogs by name and then they line up:

Now, Scouty! Now, Shnouty! Now,
Polar and Timber!

Up, Kya! Up, Kira! Up, Hunter and
Winter!"

Kirby helped Stamp hook up the sled.
"Now that they are ready, how do we
make them run?"

"You have to tell them you are ready, like
this:

To the front of the pack! Be strong and
stand tall!
Now, mush away! Mush away! Mush
away, all!"

48

The dogs pulled the sled away like a dart
and Kirby nearly fell off the back but he
held on tight. With help from Stamp,
and a lot of practice, he and the dogs
were ready to start their journey.

Early the next morning, Kirby and Stamp set out, pulled by the surprisingly strong and loyal dogs. They traveled for many days and nights until they reached a sandy beach, surrounded by palm trees that were swaying gently in the warm breeze.

"It's almost like they knew where to go," Kirby said as he began to unhook the dogs. As he looked around, Kirby saw two old, empty cabins that overlooked the ocean.

"This is the place I have been dreaming of!" Kirby shouted with joy, patting Scouty as she wagged her tail. "You may not be able to fly like reindeer, but you have your own kind of magic, don't you?" He grinned at all the eager dogs looking up at him. "You all can feel thoughts and dreams when you are really connected to someone."

Scouty tilted her head and smiled a big toothy grin, then she licked his face.

54

Kirby set up his shop just the way he liked it, with Stamp and his dogs nearby, and soon began to work on his toys. He took as long as he needed for each one to make them very special.

The story of Kirby the Elf spread to many places and over time, other elves came to join Kirby at his workshop, so they could learn how to make toys and feel the joy of giving them away to children.

DAY DREAMERS WELCOME

Kirby would always tell each person who comes to work with him, "Remember, it is not how many things you make but the joy of making and giving that is the most important thing."

Each Christmas time, Kirby packs up his dog sled with packages of special wooden toys that he made that year, and takes them to a few lucky children that he thinks will like them.

Then after a long year of making and
giving, Kirby celebrates with a big
bowl of macaroni and cheese and a
cup of apple juice, and he is happy.

Not everyone gets a gift from Kirby
the Elf to unwrap on Christmas
morning. Kirby only makes a few
each year, just the way he wants to
make them.

Kira
Hunter

If you do get one, know how much love and affection went into making it just for you.

It may not be flashy or perfect but it is special, stands out, and shines, just like you.

The End

(...Or just the beginning...)

FROM:
Kirby

"Kirby, you are an odd and wonderful elf,
and I admire you and your dream."

- Mr. C

Special Thanks to all the odd and wonderful elves that made my
dream of this book come true.

Sled Dog Team Positions:

"Now, Scouty! Now, Shnouty! Now, Polar and Timber!
Up, Kya! Up, Kira! Up, Hunter and Winter!"

Dog Dictionary:

Scouty: Labrador Retriever, Lead Dog

Friendly, eager,, and high-spirited,
Scouty is always ready for the next
adventure · after her nap.

Kiya: Siberian Husky, Team Dog

Good sense of humor and a little mischievous.
Kiya has an independent side, but she loves to
be loved.

Shnouty: Poodle, Swing Dog

Elegant, smart, and athletic,
Shnouty bounces with a self-confident prance.
She is a fierce and loyal friend.

Kira: St. Bernard, Team Dog

A sensitive and stubborn giant.
Kira is always ready for search and
rescue or to be a friend to anyone in need.

Polar: Alaskan Malamute, Swing Dog

Polar is a very strong working dog
who is always ready to play after
the work day.

Hunter: Irish Setter, Team Dog

Happy and affectionate, Hunter loves
kids and elves.
He needs a job and a routine.

Timber: German Pointer, Team Dog

Timber loves to excercise. A gentle dog,
he doesn't like to be alone and needs his
friends.

Winter: Samoyed, Wheel Dog

Extremely cuddly and playful,
Winter is also stubborn and a free spirit.

Darby: Pug, Mr. C's best friend,

Playful and energetic, Darby loves to lounge
and sit on laps.
He isn't a sled dog. but Darby is magical in
his own way.

66

67

Joe Allgeier is an inventor, toy maker, artist, and designer. He lives with his wife, son, and their dog Scout in Victor NY.

"The Legend of Kirby the Elf" is Joe's second published book. Joe is a dreamer and loves to make things out of wood like Kirby.

Joe hopes that all of his readers will follow the example of Kirby, and chase your dreams where ever they lead you.